For the girls, Jillian, Olivia, Brodie and Gwennie—MW

To Arthur and Hugo—high fliers!—AJ

Little Hare Books
8/21 Mary Street, Surry Hills
NSW 2010 AUSTRALIA

www.littleharebooks.com

Copyright © text Margaret Wild 2007
Copyright © illustrations Ann James 2007

*First published 2007
First published in paperback 2008*

National Library of Australia
Cataloguing-in-Publication entry

Author: Wild, Margaret, 1948-

Title: Lucy Goosey / authors, Margaret Wild, Ann James.

Publisher: Surry Hills, N.S.W. : Little Hare Books, 2008.

ISBN: 978 1 921272 39 4 (pbk.)

Target Audience: For primary school age.

Subjects: Courage--Pictorial works--Juvenile fiction.
Geese--Pictorial works--Juvenile fiction.

Other Authors: James, Ann.

Dewey Number: A823.4

Designed by Kerry Klinner, Megacity Design
Additional designs by Bernadette Gethings
Printed in China through Phoenix Offset

5 4 3 2 1

Lucy Goosey

Margaret Wild & Ann James

Ever since she was a fluffy gosling with flippy flappy feet, Lucy Goosey had lived in this pond.

She had jumped off that branch
sticking out of the water.

She had sat on that rock as big as a cow.

And she had played hide-and-seek in those bushes,
dark as caves.

Now Lucy Goosey was nearly full grown. She had proper feathers, and she had even learned to whiffle her wings as she landed in the pond.

'What good whiffling, Lucy Goosey!' said her mother.
'You will find it very useful during our long flight.'

'I don't want to go,' said Lucy Goosey.

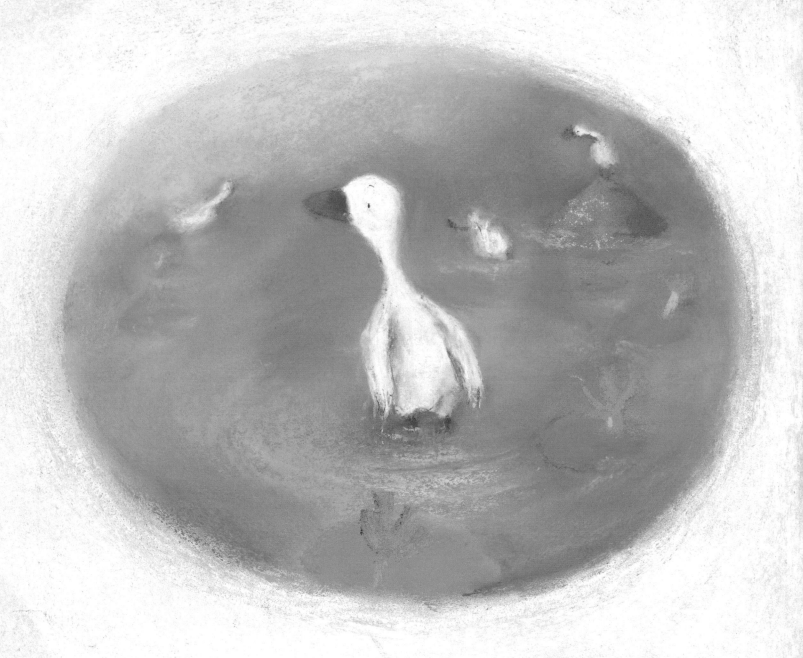

The time had come for all the geese—Lucy Goosey, her mother, her cousins, her aunties and uncles—to fly away to another country. They were leaving that very night, as soon as the sun went down.

Lucy Goosey stared up at the sky.
It was vast. Never-ending.

'I'm not going!' she said, and off she ran on her flippy flappy feet.

'Come back, Lucy Goosey,' called her mother, 'or you'll get left behind.'

'Don't care,' honked Lucy Goosey.

'Don't care,

Don't care,

Don't care!'

Lucy Goosey crept into the bushes, dark as caves.
She hid among twigs and leaves.

She tucked her head under her wing, so she couldn't
hear or see a thing.

She must have fallen asleep, because when she
squeezed out of the bushes, it was night time.
And very quiet.

Lucy Goosey hurried down to the pond.
It was empty. All the geese—even her mother!
—had gone.

Lucy Goosey swam around in lonely little circles.

Then she huddled in the reeds,
listening to leaves rustling,
twigs cracking, things slithering.

'Mum?' she whispered.

Suddenly there was the sound of wings whiffling
and a long, sad honking—'Lucy! Lucy Goosey, my dear,
where are you?'

'Mum!' said Lucy Goosey, and she sped out of the reeds faster than a flying fish.

Her mother held Lucy Goosey close. She said, 'What's the matter, Lucy Goosey? Why don't you want to leave?'

Lucy Goosey stared up at the sky.
It was dark and mysterious and never-ending.

'What if I lose my way in the misty moisty clouds?'
she asked.

'If that happens,' said her mother, 'I will search the misty moisty clouds until I find you.'

'What if I am caught in a storm
and get tossed into the tree tops?'
asked Lucy Goosey.

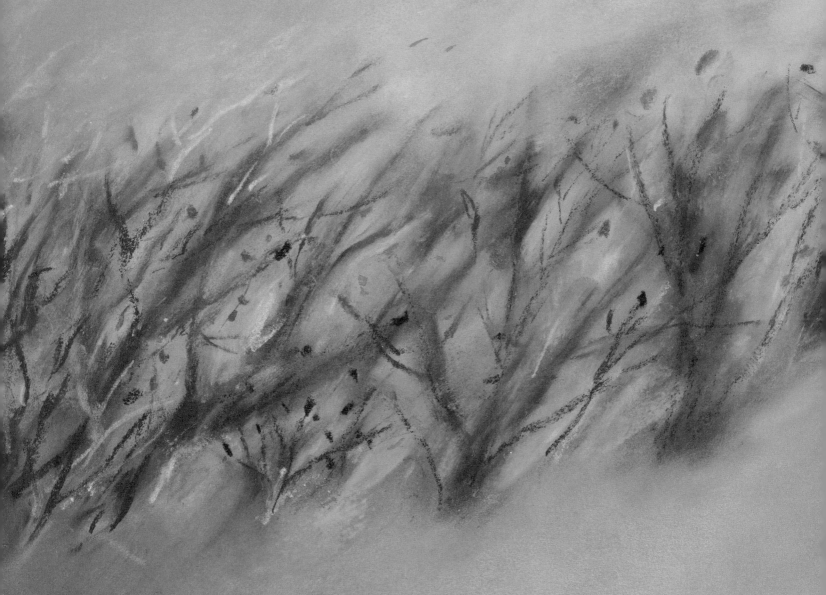

'If that happens, I will search every tree top
until I find you.'

'What if I get tired and fall into the cold, dark sea?'
asked Lucy Goosey.

'If that happens, I will search the
cold, dark sea until I find you.'

'Will you always search for me?' asked Lucy Goosey.

'Always,' said her mother.

'Even when you're *old*?'

'Even when I'm old.'

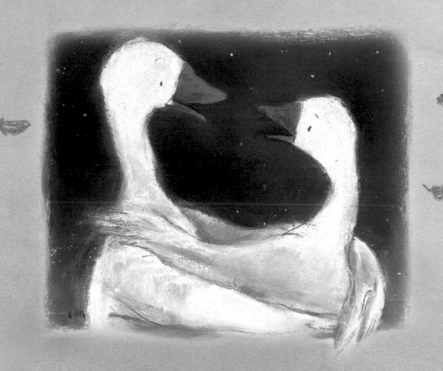

'When you're very old,' said Lucy Goosey,
'*you* might lose your way and be scared.'

'I might,' said her mother.

'If that happens,' said Lucy Goosey,
'I will look everywhere—
in the sky, on the land,
in the sea—until I find you.'

'That would be very brave of you, Lucy Goosey,' said her mother.

'Are you ready to go now?'

'Ready!' said Lucy Goosey.

And away they flew,
into a never-ending sky full of stars.